O'BRIEN flyers

'A jolly good read.'
Books Ireland

Can YOU spot the Little
Bear hidden in the story?

This book is dedicated to my Mam,
the greatest storyteller and feeder of
imagination that ever lived.

Bob Byrne is a self-taught comic artist who lives in Dublin. His comics have appeared in dozens of publications throughout the world. He enjoys drawing, playing video games, drinking too much coffee, giving out about things and shouting at the telly.

Written & illustrated by

BOB BYRNE

THE O'BRIEN PRESS
DUBLIN

First published 2006 by The O'Brien Press Ltd,
12 Terenure Road East, Rathgar, Dublin 6, Ireland.
Tel: +353 1 4923333; Fax: +353 1 4922777
E-mail: books@obrien.ie
Website: www.obrien.ie
Reprinted 2007.

ISBN: 978-1-84717-005-7

British Library Cataloguing-in-Publication Data
Byrne, Bob
Robots don't cry. - (Flyer series)
1.Robots - Juvenile fiction 2.Friendship - Juvenile fiction
3.Children's stories.
I. Title
823.9'2[J]

2 3 4 5 6 7 8 9 10
07 08 09 10

The O'Brien Press receives
assistance from

Editing, typesetting, layout, design: The O'Brien Press Ltd
Illustrations: Bob Byrne
Printed and bound in the UK by J.H. Haynes & Co Ltd,
Sparkford

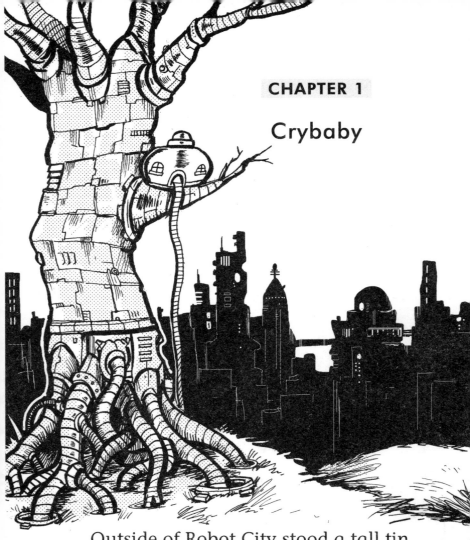

CHAPTER 1

Crybaby

Outside of Robot City stood a tall tin tree, with a small metal treehouse bolted to its side.

Inside the treehouse, four
young robots were playing
ring-toss.

Bimbot, who was the
youngest, had been waiting
a long time for his turn.

At last, Rusty handed Bimbot
a ring.

'Okay, Bimbot,' he said. 'You only
get one throw.'

Bimbot took careful aim. I'll show
them all how good I am, he thought.

He threw the ring with a mighty

WHOOOOSH!

The ring missed the hook
and bounced off the floor ...

then off the roof,
then the wall.

And then it hit
Bimbot on the head!

BONK!

Rusty burst out laughing. Klang and Klunk (who always copied Rusty), joined in.

Bimbot felt so sad that a small tear dripped from his eye.

'Leave me alone,' he cried.

Rusty stopped laughing.

'WHAT ARE YOU DOING?' he roared at Bimbot. 'Are you **CRYING**? Robots **DON'T CRY!**'

'You big baby!' said Klunk. 'Go home to your mammy!'

Poor Bimbot! He climbed down the ladder and walked away, hanging his head and staring at the ground as he went.

He walked and he walked ...

... and he walked some more.

'Why are they so mean to me?'
he said. 'I thought they were my
fr– OOPS!'

He looked around and said,
'Where am I? This isn't home.'

CHAPTER 2

Alone in the Woods

Ever since Bimbot was a baby robot he had been warned not to go into the Dark Woods.

'The Woods are full of slimy black slugs and scary blue frogs,' said the Teach-o-bot.

'There are goblins and gremlins and poisonous toadstools,' declared his dad.

'There's quicksand and stinkberries and giant sticky clingers,' said his mum.

Bimbot turned to run home,
but a creature blocked his path.

It was covered in dark fur with
a white stripe running from its
nose to its tail.

'A SKUNK!' yelled Bimbot, and he covered his nose.

The skunk looked up at him sadly.

'You don't have to do that,' he said. 'I don't smell.'

'Oh,' said Bimbot. 'That's good.'

'Not if you're a skunk,' said the skunk. 'None of the other skunks will

play with me because I don't
smell like them.'

'Oh,' said Bimbot. He knew
how that felt. 'Maybe we could
find a smell for you?'

He thought for a moment ...

'I've got it!' he said. 'There's always smelly stuff at the bottom of a well.'

'And I know where there's a well!' said the skunk excitedly.

When they reached the well, Bimbot s-t-r-e-t-c-h-e-d his arm right down and scooped up a handful of sticky slimy muck.

'Yuck!' said Bimbot.

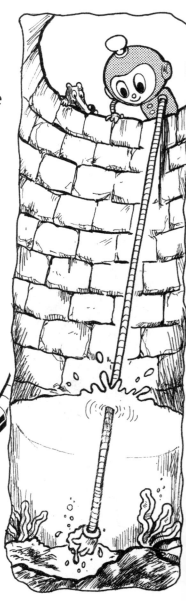

'**Yum!**' said the skunk. He rolled around in the muck until he was covered all over in slime.

'How do I smell now?' he asked.

'Like smelly socks, rotten cheese and sour milk,' said Bimbot.

'**Perfect!**' said the skunk. 'Now I smell like a *real* skunk. Thank you so much, little robot. If you ever need my help, just follow the smell.'

Well, Bimbot thought, **he** wasn't scary at all, and he walked a little bit further into the Dark Woods.

Bimbot felt a lot braver and happier after helping the skunk.

He forgot all about the mean robots back in the treehouse.

CHAPTER 3

Buzz Off!

Suddenly Bimbot heard a noise.

He stopped and listened.

'Where is that noise coming from?' he said.

A small, fuzzy bee sat on a white daisy, sobbing and sniffing loudly.

'Why are you crying?' Bimbot asked. 'You have lovely wings. You can fly. Why aren't you happy?'

'What colour am I? ' asked the little bee.

'Yellow, of course,' said Bimbot.

'Yes,' said the bee. 'Just yellow. Where are my **STRIPES**??? All the other bees have stripes. No one will play with me because I don't have stripes.'

PLIP! PLOP!

She gave such a big **SNIFF** that a daisy leaf went right up her nose.

'**ATCHOO!**'

Bimbot had an idea. He picked a ripe blackberry and squeezed it.

Then he lifted up the little bee. 'Turn around,' he instructed. As the bee turned, Bimbot painted three broad stripes on her back and tummy.

'Ooh, they're lovely,' said the bee. She flapped her wings very hard to dry her new stripes. Then she flew round and round, buzzing with delight.

BZZZZ BZZZZ BZZZZ

BZZZZ BZZZZ BZZZZ

The bee disappeared into a bush. When she came out she was carrying a big jar of honey.

'This is for you, little robot,' she said. 'You're very kind.'

'Now I must **buzz** off!'

Bimbot whistled a happy song as he skipped and hopped further into the Dark Woods.

After a while he sat down for a rest beside a clear stream.

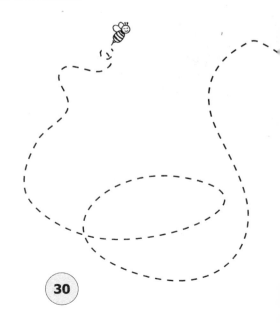

He watched frogs playing leapfrog and butterflies fluttering by.

Where are all the scary creatures everyone told me about? he wondered.

'A muh ... Muh ... **MONSTER!**'
gulped Bimbot.

CHAPTER 4

What's That?

Bimbot hid behind a rock. His metal knees were knocking together. All his nuts and bolts rattled with fear. Tears filled his eyes.

Then he thought of how Rusty,
Klunk and Klang had laughed at
him.

'Robots **DON'T CRY**,' he said
loudly. **'Ever.'**

And just to show how brave he was, instead of running away from that terrible noise, he decided to follow it.

'I'll prove I'm not a baby!'

He hopped across streams.

He ran across log bridges. He
climbed hills. He swung from
trees.

The noise grew
louder and LOUDER.

It was a **BEAR!**

A big brown bear was sitting under
a tree, growling and holding his head
in his hands.

'Hell ... Hello,
Mr Bear,' Bimbot
said nervously.
'What's wrong?'

'Promise not
to laugh?' said the
bear.

'I promise.' Bimbot
put his hand over his
little tin heart.

'You see that yummy
honey hanging from the
tree?' asked the bear. 'Well,
I **LOVE** honey, and I'm **SO**
hungry...

... but I can't climb the tree because ... because ... I'm **SCARED OF HEIGHTS**!'

'There's no need to be hungry, Mr Bear,' said Bimbot. 'Have **my** honey.'

He handed over the jar of honey that the bee had given him.

'All for me?' the bear was delighted. 'Thank you, little robot.'

He put a paw
deep in his fur
and
rummaged
around.

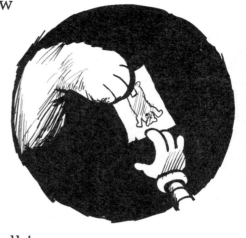

'Here,' he
handed
Bimbot a
card. 'If you
need me, just call.'

NEED A SCARE?
CALL MR. BEAR!

And off he went.

CHAPTER 5

A Really Good Idea

The sun was going down and the woods were getting cold. Bimbot decided it was time to go home.

But he didn't want to go home. Horrid Rusty and Klunk and Klang would only laugh at him again. They'd **never** believe he had been in the Dark Woods on his own!

He sat on a tree stump and thought about the friends he had made today.

PING!

He had an idea ...

He made a phone call and
whispered the details of his plan.

This was going to be FUN!

Back in the treehouse outside
Robot City, Rusty, Klunk and
Klang were still playing.

They were just finishing their
jigsaw puzzle when ...

KNOCKEDY!
KNOCK!

'Who could that be?' asked Klang.

'I bet it's that crybaby Bimbot,' said Klunk.

'Don't let him in,' said Rusty.

The knocking got louder.

'Open the door and tell him to go away,' ordered Rusty.

Klang pulled open the door, expecting to see a sad Bimbot. But there stood a **SKUNK!**

It was a really **smelly** skunk
and he wiggled his bum at Klang.

'**Yuck**!' yelled Rusty. 'That
smell! It's like stinkberries and
rotten eggs. I'm going to be sick!
Quick, open the window!'

Klunk ran to the window and threw it wide open. But instead of fresh air, a swarm of angry bees flew in.

'The trapdoor!' Rusty shouted.
'It's our only escape!'

The three robots pushed and
shoved through the trapdoor and
fell in a heap at the foot of the
tree. The bees still buzzed around
their heads.

Klang began to cry.

'Don't be such a baby,' Rusty said crossly. '**ROBOTS DON'T CRY!**'

'I'm … I'm not crying,' sniffed Klang. 'There's something in my eye.'

They didn't notice a long dark shadow creeping towards them.

Then Rusty looked up ...

'It's a **BEAR!**' he screamed.

The bear had long pointy
fangs, huge paws and razor-sharp
claws.

Rusty, Klunk and Klang were
so terrified that they couldn't
move.

'I'm scared,' Klunk sobbed.

'Me too,' howled Rusty.

'I want my Mammy,' Klang bawled.

CHAPTER 6

Robots DO Cry?

Suddenly there was silence.

The robots opened their eyes, and there stood ...

BIMBOT?

'Well, well, well,' said Bimbot. 'What have we here? Looks like Robots DO cry after all!'

'Buh-Buh-Bimbot!' cried Rusty. 'Look out! There's a big scary bear!'

'And a swarm of very angry bees!' blubbed Klunk.

'And a skunk with a smell that would fry your circuits!' yelped Klang.

'You mean my new friends?'
Bimbot laughed.

Rusty, Klunk and Klang were
astonished. They wiped their eyes
and tried to look brave.

'It's okay to cry,' Bimbot said. 'Everyone cries sometimes. When you're sad, or you're hurt, or you're frightened, it's okay to cry. Even if you're a robot.'

'You're right, Bimbot.' Rusty said. 'We're sorry we were horrible to you.'

'Will you come back to the treehouse?' he asked.

'Go on, little robot,' said the bear. 'We'll be off now. Our job is done.'

'Promise you'll come back and visit us sometime?' said the skunk.

'I promise,' said Bimbot, waving goodbye.

Back in the treehouse, all four robots played happily together until it was time to go home.

The End!